Hello, Reader!

You will like
all the funny monkeys
in this book!

Library of Congress Cataloging-in-Publication Data

Gave, Marc.
    Monkey see, monkey do / by Marc Gave; illustrated by Jacqueline Rogers.
        p.   cm. — (Hello reader)
    Summary: Rhyming text relates the antics of monkeys that play all day.
    ISBN 0-590-90748-4
    [1. Monkeys — Fiction. 2. Play — Fiction. 3. Stories in rhyme.]
    I. Rogers, Jacqueline, ill. II. Title. III. Series.
    PZ8.3.G22Mo   1993
    [E] — dc20   91-45443
                                                                                    CIP
                                                                                    AC

24 23 22 21   0 1 2/0

Printed in the U.S.A.   23

First Scholastic printing, January 1993

Monkey See, Monkey Do

by Marc Gave
Illustrated by Jacqueline Rogers

SCHOLASTIC INC. Cartwheel ·B·O·O·K·S· ®

New York   Toronto   London   Auckland   Sydney

Monkey me.
Monkey you.

Monkey see.
Monkey do.

Monkey on the left.

Monkey on the right.

Monkey in the middle.

Monkey out of sight.

Monkey up a tree.
Monkey on the ground.

Monkeys in a bunch,
monkeying around.

Monkeys stay.

Monkeys go.

Monkeys go fast.

Monkeys go slow.

Monkeys walk.

Monkeys run.

Monkeys have some monkey fun.

Monkeys bend.

Monkeys reach.

Monkeys lie
along the beach.

Monkeys swim.
Monkeys row.

Monkeys swing
to and fro.

Monkeys play
while the sky is light.

Monkeys sleep through the night.

Good night.